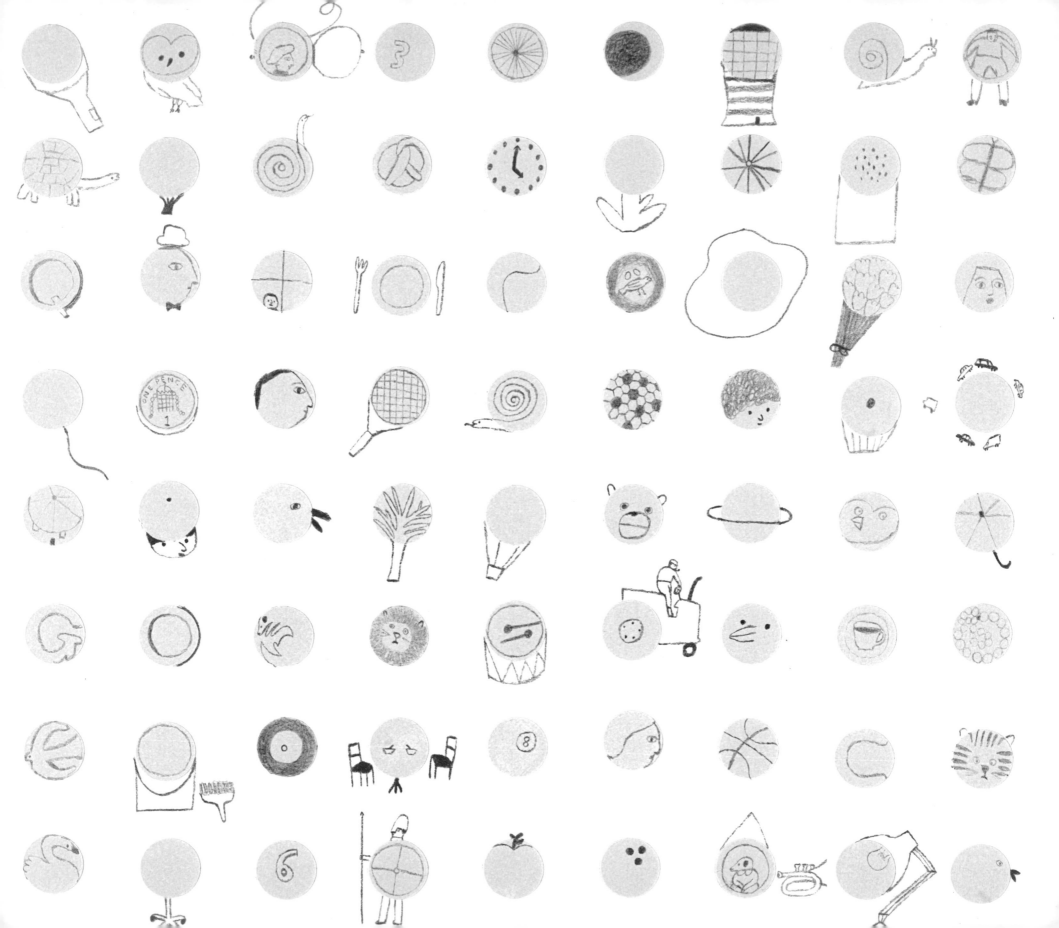

A WORLD OF YOUR OWN

by LAURA CARLIN

FOR L.J.B

Hello, this is me, Laura ...

standing in a line.
I hate standing in lines.

To make things more interesting, I imagine a World of My Own.
I'd still have lines in My World, but they might look more like this,

or this,

or this.

Let me show you how I draw and make My World by looking at what already exists.

Even in My World, I need to "GET OUT OF BED!" in the morning. But I don't want any alarm clocks — well, not any *ordinary* alarm clocks. So I like to invent different ways to start the day.

What gets you out of bed in the morning?

Could you invent an alarm clock that you can see, hear, or even smell?

To create My World, I start by looking around me.

This is my house in the real world.

First, I copy the basic shape.

Then I think of ways to make it more exciting, such as giving it a few more floors.

(That way, if friends come to stay they can have an entire floor to themselves.)

Stairs seem *really* boring,
so I add slides instead ...

and bigger windows
so I can see what's going
on outside.

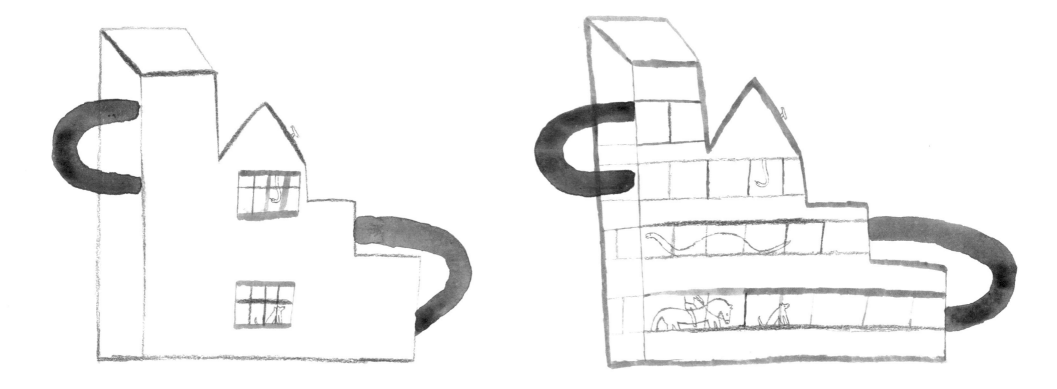

I want a swimming pool, too (obviously).

I also want my house to be high off the ground in order to look *very* important, so I put it on top of a large tree with a rope ladder for getting in and out.

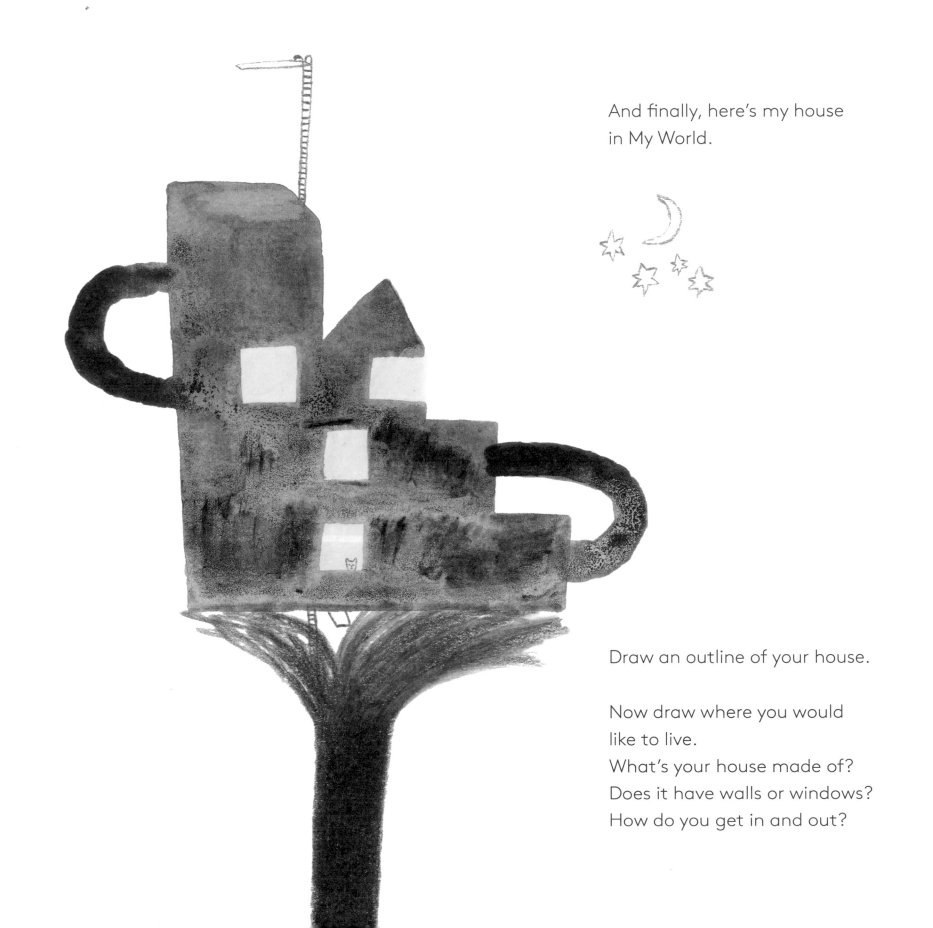

And finally, here's my house
in My World.

Draw an outline of your house.

Now draw where you would
like to live.
What's your house made of?
Does it have walls or windows?
How do you get in and out?

Next, I like to think about what kind of neighborhood my house is in.

Just like in the real world, some of the buildings
in My World look pretty dull from the outside.

But things aren't always what they seem.

Take, for example, my office supply shop, which actually sells ...

shoes for superheroes!

And this is a house on my street that really scares me,

but it's actually just full of kittens.

(Look closely: There are 131 in total.)

Inside this perfectly ordinary looking building ...

are rooms for all the people and animals I'd want to live near.

I've designed the rooms in all sorts of shapes and sizes to suit the needs of each guest. For example, a giraffe needs a tall room, a bird would like a tree to sit in, and my brother would definitely want a TV in his.

If you'd like somewhere for your friends to stay, take a piece of paper and draw blocks of different sizes.

Now, fill them with animals or people of all shapes and sizes.
Do your guests require windows, trapdoors, plants, slides, or swings?
You might want to collect different kinds of paper, material, or patterns to decorate the rooms with.

(And you'll have just made your first hotel.)

My World has other kinds of buildings
too — such as factories to make things.
In My World *all* factories have to be
the shape of whatever they make. This is
so they conform to building regulations.

This one makes pencils,

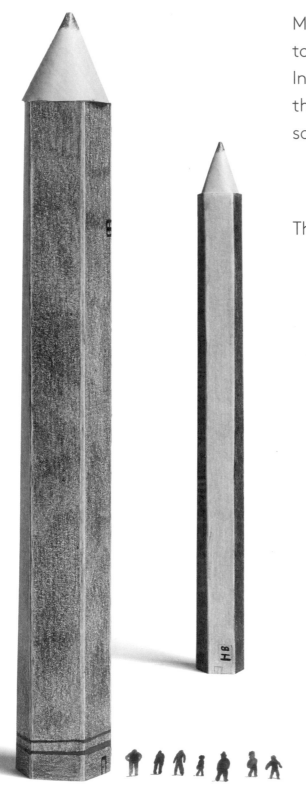

this one makes baked beans,

and this one makes spaghetti.

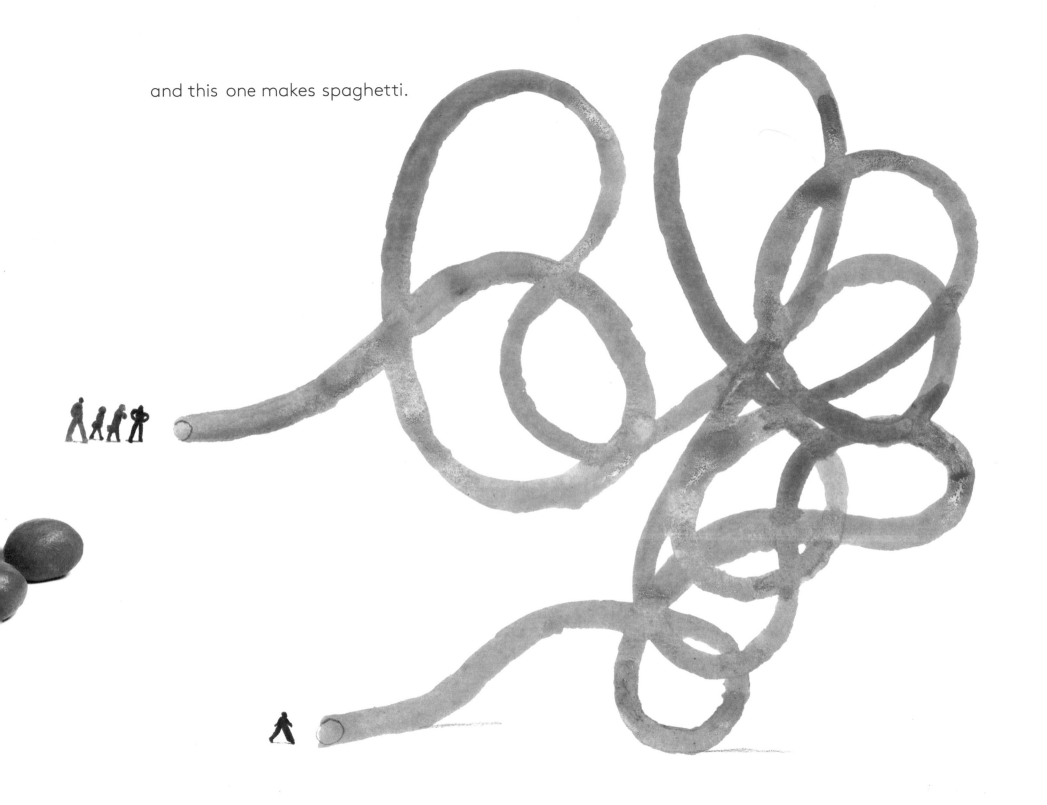

Choose three things you can't live without and imagine what the factories that make
them would look like. Do they have to be tall or short, really big or tiny?

Even in My World, you sometimes don't know what to do with the day.
So you might need some public buildings to visit. They are called
"public buildings" because everyone can go inside.

You could go to the library and borrow not only books but also toys,
hair styles, and even voices!

THE MOST **DANGEROUS REPTILE**... **EVER!**

Or, if you're brave enough, you could go and visit really dangerous animals ...

HANDS
IN
POCKETS
NO
PHOTOS
NO
TOUCHING

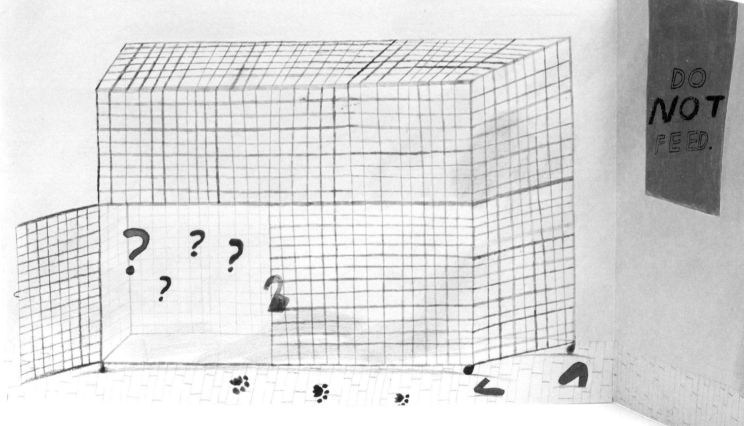

DO
NOT
FEED.

What do you like to do during the day?
What places would you like to visit?
How about a gallery of different noses or a museum
of tree houses?

Believe it or not, there's a school in My World, too.

I attend the first Tuesday of every month to learn
very important skills, such as face painting and how
to fit more than one cookie in my mouth at a time.

Here are some other lessons taught at my school.

What important things would you learn in your school?

My World not only has spectacular buildings,
it's also full of animals.

For example, everyone has a dog in My World.
Even the dogs.

I've drawn each dog differently. It makes sense
because, like us, every dog is different.

Apparently, dinosaurs became extinct millions
of years ago, so I've invited them back.

Sometimes people think my drawings of crocodiles
look like snakes, or my dogs like horses.

I prefer to see myself as an inventor.

You can be an inventor, too.
List six of your favorite animals or insects.
Draw them (or find photographs of them).

Now, by cutting them up and rearranging
them you can invent three new animals.

In the real world, we all look different from each other.
Everyone looks different in My World, too.

I draw or make them in different ways to show this:

I see a woman who's a bit shy, so I use colored pencils to draw her softly.

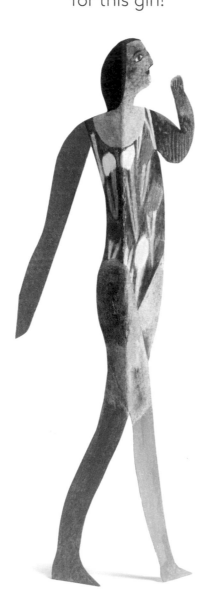

No such problem for this girl!

This man is strong and confident; he needs a solid and strong line to tell you so.

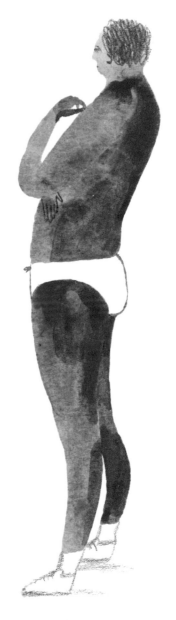

And this man is just sunburned.

This person looks a bit glum. You can tell by his hunched shoulders.

But it's ok; this boy is rushing to keep him company. And to make him look like he's in a rush, I've drawn him quickly and with energetic lines.

You can tell a lot about a person by how you draw or make them.

This is my dad. He's on a straw because he's very tall and slim.

And here's my mum who's tiny.

Granny is old and fragile and sometimes falls down,

so does my baby brother.

Now think about three people you know. How could you draw or make them to show what they look like?

It's important not to have traffic jams in My World.

(People tend to get angry in traffic jams.)

One of my favorite forms of transportation in the real world is the train.

I may as well improve the train for My World (because I can).

So, in order to get a better view, passengers are allowed to sit on the top of it.

And it can be any shape I like.

In fact, it can be the shape and size of all
my favorite animals.

What is your favorite type of transportation?

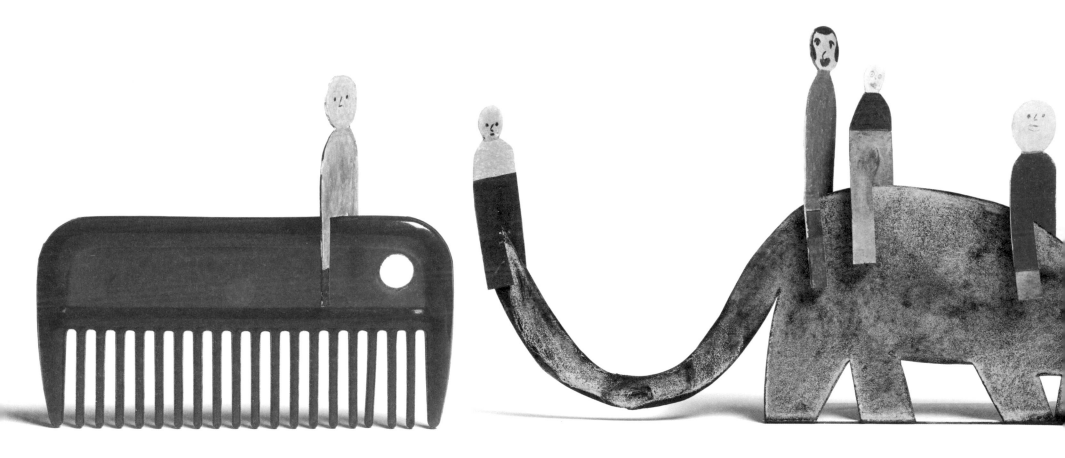

Can you think of ways to make it even better?

Before I go to bed, I look over the world I created today. I'm pretty sure friends will want to visit, so I'm going to create a flag so that My World can be seen from far away.

My flag has to represent My World so I've chosen five of my favorite things to put on it.

I also only used three colors.

(This makes it look more sophisticated.)

Tomorrow I can start again and make a whole new world.
You can start Your Own World as soon and as many times as
you like, and don't forget to look at real life for inspiration.

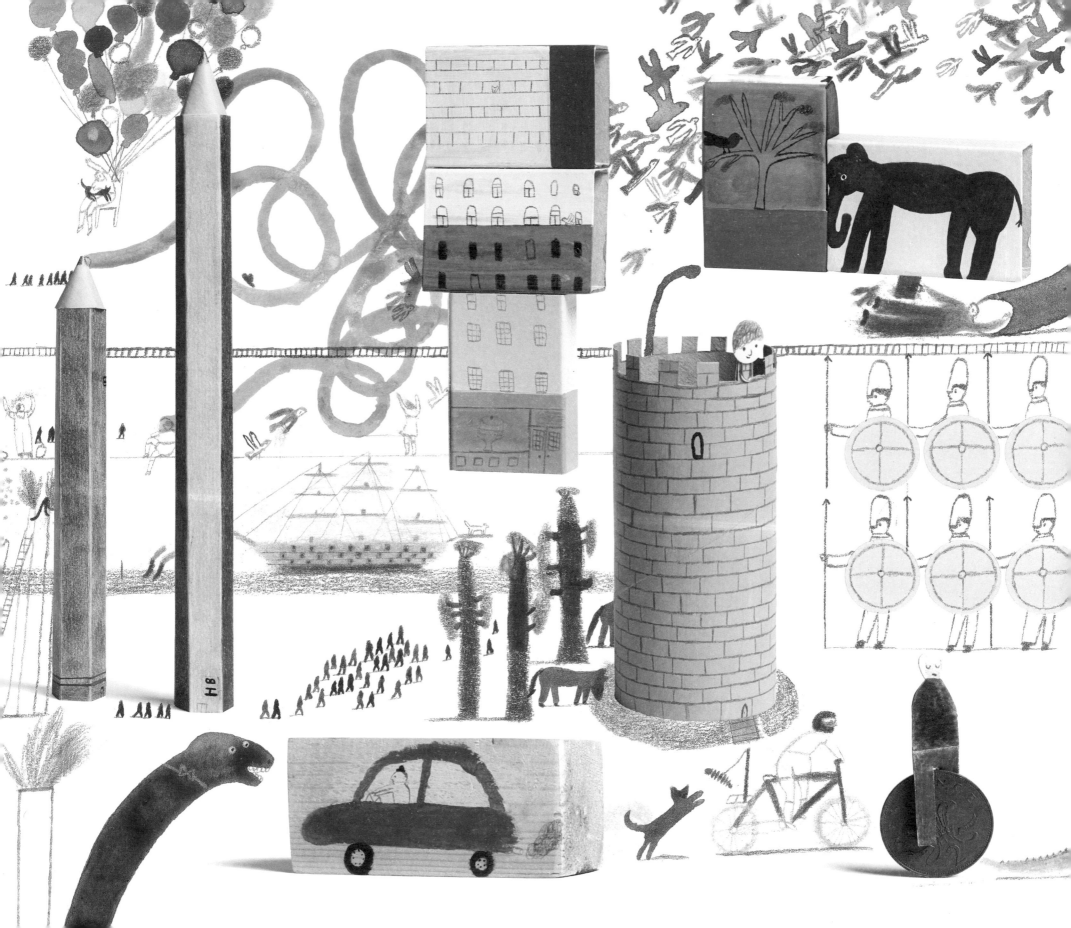

Is that a lamppost you can see outside your window?

Or a tower?

Or just an uptight snake?

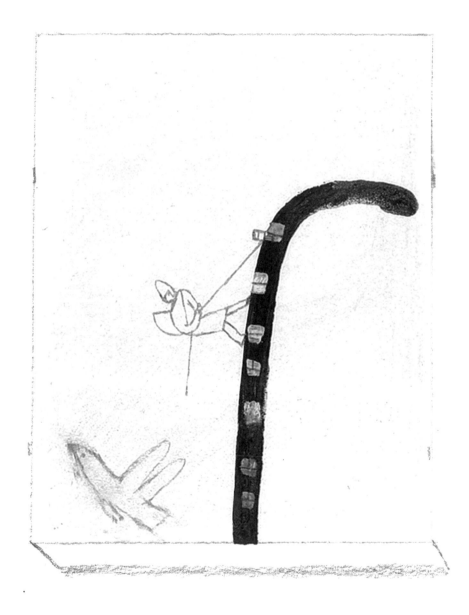

Thank you to Luke Best, Jane, Tom, and Edward
Carlin, Lucy Macintyre, and Lisa Carlin. And to
Andy Smith, Jan and Dave Hawkins, Tom and
Martha Hammick, Claudia Zeff, Jo Cartwright,
Nina Chakrabarti, Ben Branagan, Sari Easton,
Chie Miyazaki, Alexis Burgess, Mike Dempsey and
Liz Wood.

And finally to Amanda Renshaw, Rachel Williams,
Hélène Gallois Montbrun, Rebecca Price,
Sarah Boris, Dom Lee, Chiara Meattelli, Darrel
Rees, Amanda Mason, Chloe Flynn, Jenny Bull, and
to Helen Osborne.

Phaidon Press Limited
Regent's Wharf
All Saints Street
London N1 9PA

Phaidon Press Inc.
65 Bleecker Street
New York, NY 10012

www.phaidon.com

First published 2014
© 2014 Phaidon Press Limited
ISBN 978 0 7148 6362 7
007-0714

A CIP catalogue record for this book
is available from the British Library.

Commissioning Editor: Amanda Renshaw
Project Editors: Hélène Gallois Montbrun
and Rachel Williams
Production Controller: Rebecca Price

Designed by Sarah Boris
Printed in China

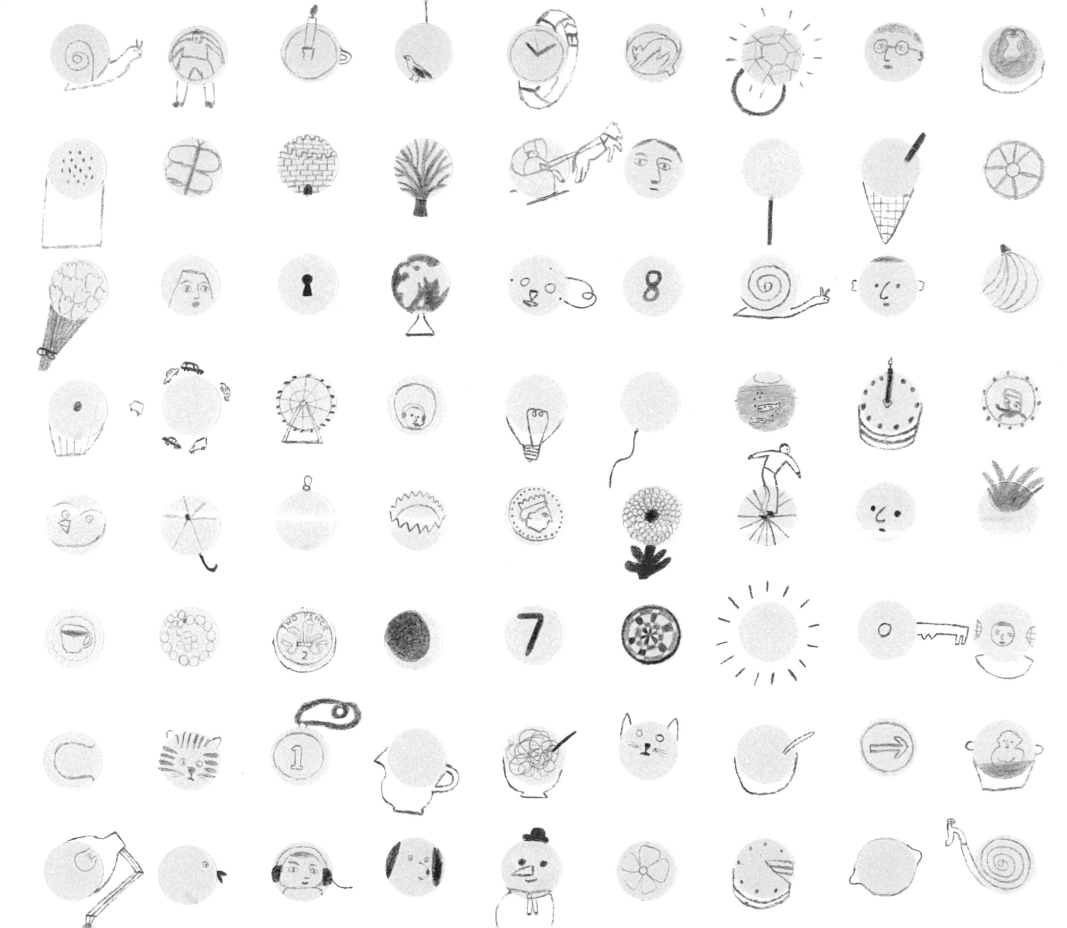

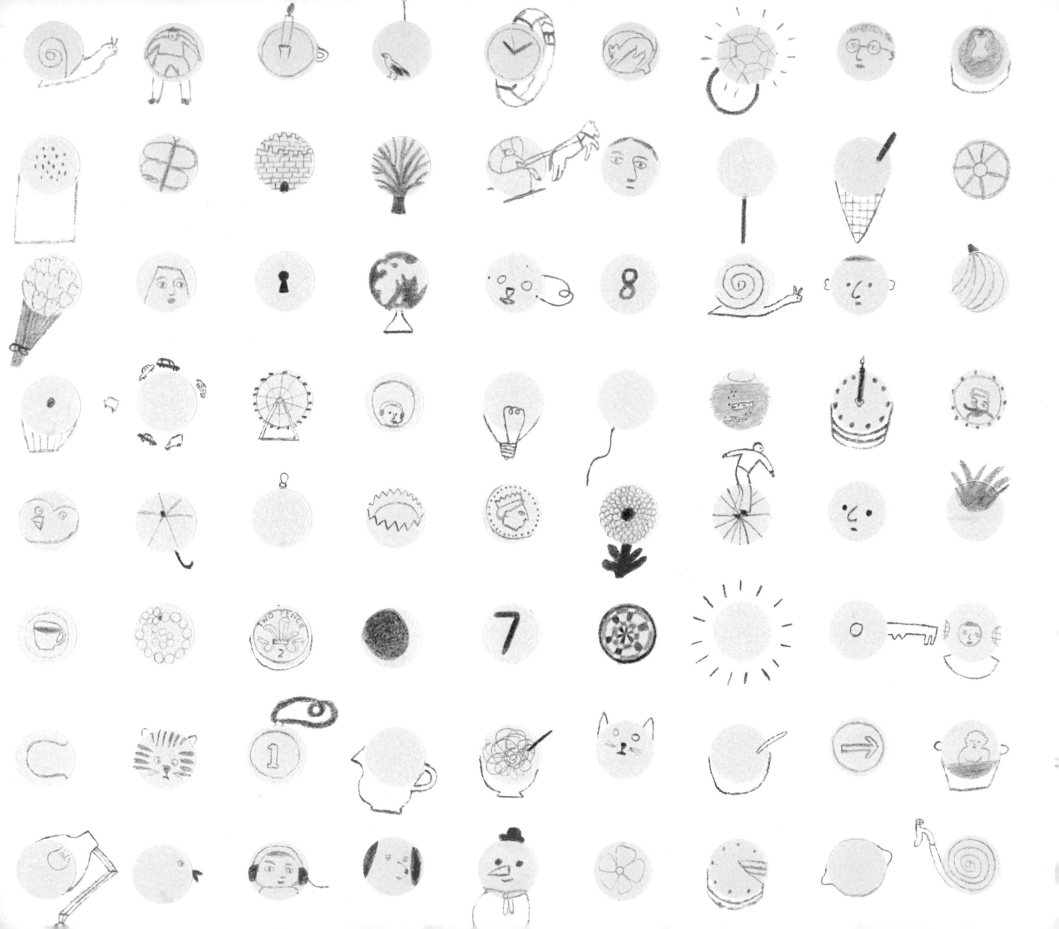